Top Pet

by Jenny Jinks and Patrick Corrigan

FRANKLIN WATTS
LONDON•SYDNEY

Miss Timms had something to tell the class.

"Next week is Pet Week," she said. "Every day one of you will bring your pet to school and tell us about it. At the end of the week, you will all vote for the Top Pet."

Everyone was very excited.
Kobi was excited too.

St. Helens Libraries

Please return / renew this item by the last date shown. Items may be renewed by phone and internet.

Telephone: (01744) 676954 or 677822
Email: centrallibrary@sthelens.gov.uk
Online: sthelens.gov.uk/librarycatalogue

STHLibraries   sthlibrariesandarts   STHLibraries

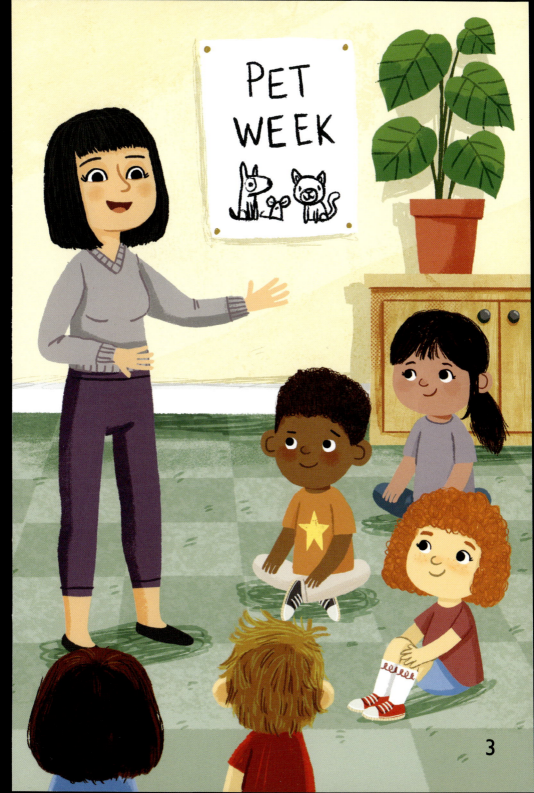

3

On Monday, Megan brought
her mouse into school.

"This is Milo," she said. "He can run
very fast."

Milo sped around the classroom
in his ball.

On Tuesday, Rachel brought
her puppy into school.
"This is Patch. He can do tricks."
"Roll over, Patch," said Rachel,
and Patch rolled over.

On Wednesday, Alex brought
his cat into school.
"This is Coco. She likes to curl up
and sleep in the sun."
Coco curled up on the window sill
and slept all day.

On Thursday, Samia brought
her pony into school.

"This is Rango. He likes
to eat apples."
Everyone had a go riding Rango
around the playground.

On Friday, it was Kobi's turn.

"Where is your pet?"

asked Megan.

Everyone looked at Kobi.

"Come with me," said Kobi.

Kobi took the class outside ...

and down the road ...

and round the corner.

"Where are we going?"

everyone said.

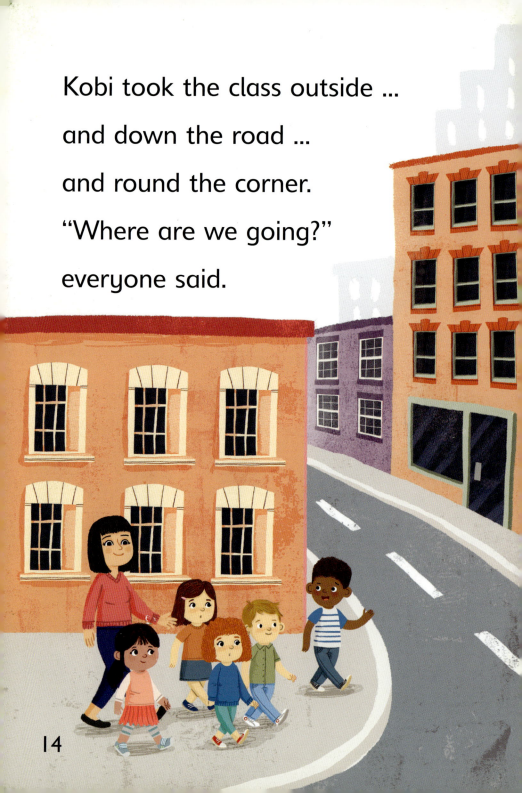

They came to the zoo and

Kobi took them all inside.

"This is Leo the monkey,"
Kobi said. "I visit him every week
and help my mum to look after him.
He likes to sit on my head."

Everyone stared at Leo the monkey.
Then they smiled at Kobi.

17

"What a great pet!" everyone cried.
They all wanted to help look after
a monkey at the zoo too.

"Top Pet goes to Kobi's monkey, Leo!" they all said.

Story order

Look at these 5 pictures and captions.
Put the pictures in the right order
to retell the story.

1

Leo the monkey is Top Pet.

2

Rachel brings Patch to school.

3

The class comes to the zoo.

4

Miss Timms talks about Pet Week.

5

Samia brings Rango to school.

21

Independent Reading

This series is designed to provide an opportunity for your child to read on their own. These notes are written for you to help your child choose a book and to read it independently.

In school, your child's teacher will often be using reading books which have been banded to support the process of learning to read. Use the book band colour your child is reading in school to help you make a good choice. *Top Pet* is a good choice for children reading at Orange Band in their classroom to read independently.

The aim of independent reading is to read this book with ease, so that your child enjoys the story and relates it to their own experiences.

About the book

It's Pet Week at school, and the children will vote for whose pet is the best. Kobi can't bring his pet into school, but he can bring his class to the zoo to meet his special pet. Everyone agrees Kobi has the Top Pet!

Before reading

Help your child to learn how to make good choices by asking:
"Why did you choose this book? Why do you think you will enjoy it?"
Look at the cover together and ask: "What do you think the story will be about?" Ask your child to think of what they already know about the story context. Then ask your child to read the title aloud. Establish that in this book, there will be some interesting pets.
Ask: "What do you know about having a pet at home? What kinds of pets do you like best?"
Remind your child that they can sound out the letters to make a word if they get stuck.
Decide together whether your child will read the story independently or read it aloud to you.

During reading

Remind your child of what they know and what they can do independently. If reading aloud, support your child if they hesitate or ask for help by telling the word. If reading to themselves, remind your child that they can come and ask for your help if stuck.

After reading

Support comprehension by asking your child to tell you about the story. Use the story order puzzle to encourage your child to retell the story in the right sequence, in their own words. The correct sequence can be found at the bottom of the next page.

Help your child think about the messages in the book that go beyond the story and ask: "Why can't Leo the monkey go to school with Kobi?"

Give your child a chance to respond to the story: "Did you have a favourite part? Did you think Leo was Top Pet too or did you prefer a different pet from the story? Why/why not?"

Extending learning

Help your child understand the story structure by using the same sentence patterning and adding different elements. "Let's make up a new story about interesting animals. What kind of habitat will the animals live in? What will the animals be competing for and who will vote for the winner?"

In the classroom, your child's teacher may be teaching adding the suffix -ed to the end of verbs, to make the simple past tense. There are many examples in this book that you could look at with your child, for example: *rolled, curled, looked, wanted.*

Find these together and point out the root word and suffix each time.

Franklin Watts
First published in Great Britain in 2020
by The Watts Publishing Group

Copyright © The Watts Publishing Group 2020

Series Editors: Jackie Hamley, Melanie Palmer and Grace Glendinning
Series Advisors: Dr Sue Bodman and Glen Franklin
Series Designer: Peter Scoulding

A CIP catalogue record for this book is
available from the British Library.

ISBN 978 1 4451 7094 7 (hbk)
ISBN 978 1 4451 7096 1 (pbk)
ISBN 978 1 4451 7095 4 (library ebook)

Printed in China

Franklin Watts
An imprint of
Hachette Children's Group
Part of The Watts Publishing Group
Carmelite House
50 Victoria Embankment
London EC4Y 0DZ

An Hachette UK Company
www.hachette.co.uk

www.franklinwatts.co.uk

Answer to Story order: 4, 2, 5, 3, 1